ANN'
INVA

ANN'S WAR
INVASION

Hannah Howe

Goylake Publishing

Goylake Publishing, Iscoed, 16A Meadow Street, North Cornelly, Bridgend, Glamorgan. CF33 4LL

ISBN: 978-1-9999619-0-9

Printed and bound in Britain by Imprint Digital, Exeter, EX5 5HY

To my family, with love

CHAPTER ONE

Ann Morgan forced her spade into the dry ground and turned the soil. Then she paused to admire the vegetables in her allotment. A combination of warm summer sunshine and frequent showers had served the vegetables well and, this year, she would harvest a good crop.

The sound of aeroplanes, flying overhead, captured Ann's attention. The aeroplanes, an Avro Anson and a Westland Lysander, were on a training mission, from nearby Stormy Down.

As the aeroplanes flew along the coast, Ann thought about Emrys, her husband of seven months, and the day he had embarked upon his top secret mission. That day, 24th March 1944, weighed heavily on her mind, for on that day the Nazis had shot down his aeroplane, somewhere over France.

Emrys' missions, for the RAF, were top secret; therefore, Ann knew little about them. However, Charles Montagu, a spymaster and Emrys' boss, had offered her titbits of information, possibly as a balm to ease her anguish, as a liniment to soothe her troubled mind. Ann had received no word from Emrys, yet she held on to the hope that he was still alive.

According to Charles Montagu, Emrys had embarked upon a reconnaissance mission, to gather intelligence for the big push, the day the Allies would land in France, the day they would seek to drive the Nazi invaders out of that country and liberate Europe. That day had arrived six weeks ago, on the 6th June 1944. Now, it could be only a matter of time before the American soldiers, who had been training on the local beaches and sand dunes for the past nine months, joined the second wave and landed in Normandy.

Ann removed a selection of vegetables from her allotment, including potatoes, carrots, onions, cabbages and swedes. She would take these surplus vegetables to the local Women's Institute for redistribution.

With the vegetables secure in a hessian sack, Ann washed her hands and changed her clothes. Then she glanced into her bedroom mirror to admire her knee-length Utility dress. Of course, due to austerity measures, buttons and pleats, and the length of hemlines, were all severely restricted. Nevertheless, Ann considered that the short-sleeved green dress, with its matching felt hat and thin leather belt, suited her well.

From her bedroom, Ann ran downstairs. There she loaded her sack into the Jensen, a smart, sporty car, a perk of Emrys' trade. Ann reflected on the Jensen. The RAF had not reclaimed the car so surely that hinted at hope; surely the RAF had received word, maybe a secret coded message, a cipher which stated that Emrys was still alive? Ann sighed. Maybe she was being fanciful. Maybe she was clutching at straws. If so, let it be, for she had nothing else to cling on to.

Ann drove south, three miles along the coast, from her home in Kenfig to the seaside town of Porthcawl. There, she parked on the seafront. Before calling at the Women's Institute, she entered Trevor Bowman's office. Before his brutal murder, Trevor Bowman had been a private investigator while Ann had served as his secretary. The lease on the office ran for another year, so Ann called in to check for messages and to tidy up the last vestiges of paperwork. In truth, this was a light task and Ann told herself that she really must move on. However, something compelled her to stay, maybe a connection with the past, maybe a fanciful, vague notion about the future.

From Trevor Bowman's office, Ann walked along John Street, the main street in Porthcawl, towards the Women's Institute. Inside the Institute, she found much merriment as the senior members tried out a new gizmo, supplied by the American soldiers. The gizmo was a simple press that canned food.

Ann smiled as Enid, a spritely lady in her mid-sixties, pressed a lever; the lever rotated a turntable, which sealed the can. Applause broke out, followed by laughter.

Ann delivered her vegetables and talked with the ladies. Then she stepped out of the building, into the sunshine.

Outside, Ann turned a corner, only to bump into Violet Hopkins, a woman in her early fifties. Violet was riding her bicycle, a relic from the Edwardian age.

"Sorry," Violet apologized with a round of nervous laughter.

"Nothing broken," Ann said. She glanced down and straightened the hem on her dress.

Ann knew Violet as an acquaintance, through the Women's Institute. A farmer's wife of slight build and medium height, she possessed a rash of freckles, fine auburn hair, tied into a bun, a slightly crooked nose and vibrant violet eyes.

"Mrs Morgan," Violet said.

"Ann," Ann said.

"Ann. Do you have a minute?"

"But of course."

The ladies walked along John Street, Ann clutching her handbag while Violet pushed her bicycle. As they walked, they spied a poster on a billboard. The poster advertised the film *Penitentiary* starring Walter Connolly, John Howard and Jean Parker, which dated from 1938, before the war. In those days, new films appeared in the local cinemas every week, whereas now film buffs had to make do with recycled films.

After gazing at the gaudy poster, Violet said, "I heard that you're thinking of taking over Mr Bowman's office and becoming a private detective."

"Where did you hear that?" Ann laughed.

"At the Institute," Violet said, "around town."

"At the moment, I'm just tidying up loose ends," Ann explained, "then I'll move on."

"But you do know something about detective work," Violet persisted.

"Only what I've gleaned from Mr Bowman," Ann said. She paused outside an Italian café. Through Mussolini, the Italians had sided with Hitler. However, the locals still regarded the Italian cafés, and their owners, with some affection. "Why do you ask?" Ann smiled.

"It's my daughter," Violet said, "Adeline." The farmer's wife gripped the handlebars on her bicycle and stared at the ground. "She's gone missing."

"Missing?" Ann frowned.

"Yes." Violet removed her right hand from the handlebars. With nervous fingers, she tugged at a loose thread, which dangled from her knitted cardigan.

"Has this happened before?" Ann asked.

"When things get heated at home," Violet said,

"Adeline takes herself off and disappears for a day or two."

"Where does she go?"

"I don't know," Violet said; "she never tells me." Her fingers became more frantic as she tugged at the loose thread. "She's been gone four days this time, and I'm worried."

"Could you explain," Ann asked, "what you mean by, 'when things get heated at home'?"

"Adeline argues with her father. He's very strict and demanding. He wants her to be the perfect daughter, and sometimes she can't cope."

"And when the pressure builds, she disappears for a day or two?"

"That's right," Violet said. "But she always returns."

"Only this time it's been four days."

"Yes," Violet said. She risked a quick glance at Ann. Then, aware that she was shredding her cardigan, she released the loose thread. "I was wondering if you could ask around, discretely, of course."

"I could do that," Ann said.

"Thank you," Violet sighed, her relief palpable.

Ann paused while a nurse in a Red Cross uniform strolled towards the butchers, a ration book clutched in her left hand. The nurse would have meat for dinner and Ann wondered, idly, what she would prepare for her evening meal – probably a salad, because the tomatoes and cucumbers were doing well in the greenhouse.

Ann and Violet walked on. Then Ann asked, "Are you sure Adeline's in hiding because of your husband?"

"What else could it be?" Violet frowned, the furrows on her freckled forehead deepening.

"Does she have a boyfriend?" Ann asked.

"Not that I know of. Stanley, my husband, disapproves, you see; he reckons she's not old enough; she's only twenty-two."

"Maybe she has a secret boyfriend," Ann suggested.

"She goes to the dances," Violet said.

"Maybe she met someone there?"

Ann paused to consider Violet's reaction. Although she was trying to comfort the woman, the deepening frown on her forehead suggested that she was adding to her woes.

"I will ask around," Ann said. "Don't worry; I'm sure Adeline will turn up somewhere."

CHAPTER TWO

Ann spent the afternoon wandering around town, casually mentioning Adeline Hopkins' name whenever the opportunity presented itself. People smiled when Ann mentioned Adeline's name, which suggested that they liked her. Ann knew Adeline, but only in passing; she had no great knowledge of the young woman.

From her conversations, Ann discovered that Adeline loved dancing, music and nature. And, apparently, she could be something of a flirt.

With her legs weary, Ann returned home. She parked the Jensen then wandered into the sand dunes, to sit on a grassy knoll and admire the view. The sand dunes were a good place, Ann reckoned, a good place to clear your mind and connect with nature.

In the distance, she noticed the American soldiers from the 28th Infantry Division, milling around, performing their duties at their makeshift army camp. Even from a distance, she noticed an extra edge to the camp, a build up of tension. Without doubt, the soldiers would be leaving soon, some never to return. The town would be quiet without them. More to the point, would they face another Dunkirk, or push on into Germany?

Butterflies fluttered by. A bee settled on a dark

red orchid while birds swooped towards the large freshwater pool. The scene offered a sense of tranquillity, until the groans of aeroplane engines rumbled overhead as trainee pilots, gunners and navigators completed their daily manoeuvres.

Ann placed a hand to her forehead, to shield her eyes. She studied the aeroplanes. Then a figure entered her peripheral vision. She turned and gazed at Detective Inspector Max Deveraux, the police officer who had led the enquiry into Trevor Bowman's murder. As Deveraux approached, Ann smiled; she liked the man and was pleased to see him.

Ann stood then walked towards Max Deveraux. A widower in his early thirties, Deveraux possessed soft brown eyes, wavy brown hair and a strong, square jaw. Muscular and clean-shaven, he walked with a slight limp, favouring his right leg. He carried shrapnel in that leg, a legacy of his army service and the retreat from Dunkirk.

Deveraux removed his trilby and rolled the hat between his fingers. His fingers were forever busy, Ann noted; she speculated, maybe this was another legacy of his war service. He nodded towards Ann then said, "I thought I'd see how you're getting on."

"I'm doing well," Ann smiled, "thank you."

"Any word about your husband?"

"No," Ann said, her tone heavy, burdened with

sadness, "nothing, yet."

Deveraux nodded. He glanced down to the sand. With a thoughtful look on his face, he spun his trilby around on his right index finger. Looking up, he said, "The situation is chaotic over there; it would be difficult for him to get word back to you. But he's safe; I have no proof; call it an old copper's instinct."

"I hope you're right," Ann said.

Deveraux offered Ann an encouraging smile then they lapsed into silence.

As they walked through the sand dunes, Deveraux asked, "What are you up to?"

"I'm tidying up a few loose ends at Mr Bowman's office. And I'm looking for a young woman."

"Oh." Deveraux paused. He placed his trilby on his head and adjusted the brim. Then his fingers reached for a leafy fern and caressed its fronds. "Who?" he asked, his tone loaded with interest.

"Adeline Hopkins. She's twenty-two. She lives with her parents at Marshfield Farm, near Nottage. Her disappearance may be connected to an argument with her father, or maybe she has a secret boyfriend." Ann paused. She glanced at Max Deveraux and asked, "Where should I start?"

"What are her interests?"

"From what I've gathered, I'd say nature, music

and dancing."

"Then try the dance halls," Deveraux suggested. "If I were you, I'd start there."

"Thank you, Max," Ann smiled; "I'll do that."

The sound of aeroplane engines drew their attention to the sky. While a Lysander target tug streamed its target over the coast, a Whitley bomber followed in its wake. As directed, the trainee gunner in the Whitley opened fire, aiming for the long, windsock target. However, Deveraux sensed that something was amiss. He screamed, "His guns have jammed! Get down!"

Taking Ann's breath away, Deveraux pushed her on to the ground. They rolled down a sand dune. At the bottom of the dune, he climbed on top of her. She gasped as bullets riddled the sand, as the murderous line sprayed grains into their faces, over their clothes and into their hair.

The aeroplanes flew out to sea. All fell quiet. In the silence, Ann could hear the beating of her heart; she could smell Deveraux's aftershave and hair gel, an attractive aroma. She felt the weight of his manly presence and the protective strength of his powerful arms. She felt safe, secure. The danger had passed.

"Are you all right?" Deveraux asked. He rolled on to the sand and searched for his trilby. He located the hat and a packet of playing cards. The playing cards had fallen from his coat pocket, along with his notebook and pen.

"My legs are like jelly," Ann said, standing, resting her weight against Max Deveraux. "But I'm okay." She paused and took a deep breath. "Thank you," she added with a grateful smile. "You saved my life. How can I repay you?"

Deveraux placed the playing cards, his notebook and pen into his coat pockets. He brushed the sand from his trilby. "I'm sure you'll think of something," he said, his lips twitching into a lazy smile. Then, with a straight face, he added, "Let me walk you home, out of harm's way."

At the garden gate, the entrance to Ann's Homestead cottage, Deveraux paused and asked, "Are you sure you're okay?"

"I'm fine," Ann said. "And thank you again."

Deveraux nodded. He adjusted his trilby. Then with a solicitous word and a painful limp, he hobbled away. "Take care," he said. "I'll see you around."

CHAPTER THREE

That night, Ann visited the dance halls, in particular the Pavilion in Porthcawl. Clothed in a satin, pre-war dress, she mingled with the dancers, mainly local women and embedded American soldiers. She listened to the jazz band, admired the dancers and asked questions about Adeline Hopkins. She also recalled a wedding reception, the evening when she had first set eyes on Emrys. It was love at first sight; he introduced her to the foxtrot and they danced the night away. After a brief courtship, they married, and Ann had never felt happier. How she longed for a return to those days.

Through chatting with a saxophone player, Ann discovered that Adeline had a boyfriend, Richard Lyall, a trainee gunner at Stormy Down. She recalled the incident on the sand dunes, the faulty guns, and shivered. Max had saved her life. How could she repay him? She would think of a way.

The following morning, Ann travelled five miles inland, to Stormy Down, to talk with Richard Lyall in connection with Adeline Hopkins.

Ann parked the Jensen outside the main gate and stated her business to the guard on sentry duty. First, he checked her identity card. Then he allowed her into the camp. Indeed, he was kind enough to direct her towards Richard Lyall.

To Ann's mind, the camp resembled a small village, a multi-cultural hamlet built exclusively for the war. She walked past WAAF quarters, married quarters, a church, a cinema and a school. She heard a variety of accents – French, Canadian, Indian, Czechoslovakian, Polish and more.

At the airfield, Ann found Richard Lyall. He was standing beside his Whitley bomber, examining the fuselage. In his early twenties, and of stocky build, he had close-cropped black hair, slicked with hair cream, and a bent, boxer's nose. His lips were full and puckered while a scar scribed an arc under his right eye.

Ann approached then asked, "Richard Lyall?"

"That's right," he said. "Who wants to know?"

"My name is Ann Morgan. I'm a private investigator." Ann paused. Was she really a private investigator? Had she really said those words? After some thought, she concluded that she would go along with that statement and not bring Trevor Bowman's name into the conversation and rake over the past. She continued, "I wonder...could I ask you some questions?"

"Fire away," Richard Lyall said, his tone bright and breezy.

"Is this your aeroplane?" Ann asked, her gaze taken by the impressive, imposing structure.

"It is," Lyall said.

"Do you have a problem with the guns?"

"They jammed," he conceded, "yesterday."

"You nearly shot me," Ann scowled, "on Kenfig sand dunes."

"Sorry about that," he laughed. "But the problem's solved now; all clear."

Although Ann took Richard Lyall at his word, she retreated, mindful of the guns. While he wiped his hands on an oily rag, she said, "I understand that you were walking out with Adeline Hopkins."

"I was," he replied cautiously, his fingers squeezing the rag.

"But no longer?"

"That's right," Lyall said.

"May I ask why?" Ann enquired. She smiled sweetly and canted her head to her left, her innocent look designed to suppress all suspicion.

However, Lyall was a man of the world; he sensed danger and frowned. "What's it to you?" he asked.

"I'm looking for Adeline," Ann said, "on behalf of her mother."

He shook his head and scoffed. "She's done a moody again?"

"It seems so," Ann said.

"I'm sorry to hear that," Lyall said, "but I haven't seen her for about a week."

They paused while an aeroplane, an Avro Anson, prepared to land. The airfield at Stormy Down was short, approximately a thousand yards, and grassy, and therefore not ideally suited to its task. The Avro Anson bounced and wobbled as its wheels encountered the ruts made by previous aircraft. However, displaying considerable skill, the pilot brought the aeroplane safely home.

Ann turned her attention back to Richard Lyall. She asked, "How did you meet Adeline?"

"Before I became a trainee gunner, I worked on her father's farm."

"But you're no longer close to Adeline?"

"She prefers the GIs," Lyall said. Once again, his fingers tightened around the oily rag and with his knuckles showing he threatened to tear it apart. "She ditched me."

"She's romantically attached to an American soldier?"

"I guess so," he said through clenched teeth. "I think his name is Glenn Hendry, or Henley."

"How do you feel about that?" Ann asked.

In a burst of violent emotion, Lyall threw the rag on to the ground. "I feel gutted," he said. "When she told me, I had words with her."

"Did you speak with the soldier, Glenn Henley?"

"We met and I expressed my opinion, yeah."

"How did he take it?" Ann asked.

"He punched me."

"And your reaction?"

"I punched him back."

At first, Ann frowned. Then she pictured the brawl and tried to smile. "Aren't we supposed to be on the same side?"

"When fighting the Nazis, yeah. But we have a duty to stand up for our own girls."

Lyall retrieved his oily rag from the dusty ground. He walked away from his Whitley bomber, towards the firing range, maybe to let off more steam. Mindful of the rutted ground and her heeled shoes, Ann followed – I really must wear something more sensible, she told herself, maybe my flat brogues.

Ann joined Richard Lyall outside the firing range. There, she said, "If you should see Adeline, or hear anything about her, would you please contact me?"

She delved into her handbag and produced an old business card. With a ballpoint pen, she crossed out Trevor Bowman's name and inscribed her own. Maybe I should have some new cards printed, she thought.

Lyall studied the business card then nodded. "Sure," he said.

"And the guns on your aeroplane," Ann said,

"are you certain that they're safe now?"

"They're as safe as houses," Lyall said, "unless you happen to be siding with Hitler."

With that comforting thought in mind, Ann returned to the Jensen to ponder her next move. She considered her options. Then she drove to the army camp at Kenfig, to talk with the GIs.

CHAPTER FOUR

With a wary eye cast to the sky, and the Stormy Down aeroplanes, Ann walked through the sand dunes to the army camp in search of liaison officer Lieutenant Mike Zabrinski.

As Ann walked, she spied numerous tanks, jeeps and DUKWs, the infantry division's amphibious vehicles. She also spied hundreds of men in their smart barathea uniforms decorated with Red Indian corps flashes.

When the Americans arrived, in October 1943, Lieutenant Zabrinski conducted a lecture at the Prince of Wales Inn, principally to win over the support of the locals. Ann had attended that lecture; therefore, she was vaguely familiar with Lieutenant Zabrinski. She recognized him as a tall man with handsome, regular features, playful blue eyes and short dark hair. During the lecture, he had revealed that his parents were in the catering business, a business he hoped to return to, after the war.

Ann waited until the lieutenant stood alone. Then she approached him and said, "Lieutenant Zabrinski."

He smiled, displaying a set of even white teeth. "How may I help you, ma'am?"

"My name is Ann Morgan, Mrs Ann Morgan. I'm a private investigator."

"Really," Lieutenant Zabrinski said.

"Yes, I am," Ann said, more to convince herself than the lieutenant. "I'm looking for a runaway, a young woman, Adeline Hopkins."

Lieutenant Zabrinski glanced at the barracks, at the soldiers and the vehicles. He said, "And you expect to find her in this camp?"

"Not exactly," Ann said. "But I was wondering if you'd seen her."

"Sorry," the lieutenant said, "I don't know anyone of that name."

"I believe that Adeline was walking out with one of your men," Ann said, "Sergeant Glenn Henley."

Lieutenant Zabrinski turned on his well-polished heels. For the first time, Ann had captured his full attention. Ignoring the military milieu, which swirled all around, he led her towards a quiet corner of the sand dunes.

"Adeline Hopkins and her connection to Sergeant Henley, that is a coincidence," he said.

"Is it?" Ann frowned.

"Yes, it is," Lieutenant Zabrinski said, "because I'm looking for Sergeant Henley."

Ann's beautiful blue eyes widened. She said, "Sergeant Henley's disappeared?"

"He's gone AWOL," Lieutenant Zabrinski said. "He's been missing, four days."

"Maybe he's with Adeline?" Ann mused.

"Maybe he is." Lieutenant Zabrinski paused. With a thoughtful look on his face, he caressed the dimple in his chin. "Then again..." he shrugged.

"Do you think Sergeant Henley disappeared because of the imminent invasion?"

"What invasion?" Lieutenant Zabrinski scowled.

"Well," Ann said, "with all the recent troop activity, I assumed..."

Zabrinski's scowl deepened. "Please, ma'am," he said, "keep your assumptions to yourself. Careless talk costs lives."

"I'm not a rumour-monger," Ann said; "I don't spread gossip with everyone."

Ann and Lieutenant Zabrinski turned their backs as a gust of wind whipped up the sand and blew it into their faces. On stormy days, the wind whistled in from the Severn Sea and those storms, over many centuries, had created the sand dunes. Ann shook the sand from her honey-blonde hair – I should have worn a headscarf, she reasoned.

"Maybe you have a point," Lieutenant Zabrinski said, the breeze tugging at his barathea uniform; "maybe Sergeant Henley is with your Adeline Hopkins."

"Maybe they've eloped," Ann said. "But to return to an earlier point and to explore another possibility; do you think Sergeant Henley went AWOL because of the imminent invasion?"

"No, I don't," Lieutenant Zabrinski said, his tone firm, resolute.

"Why do you say that?" Ann asked.

"Because I know my men; Henley is not that type."

"You have men looking for Sergeant Henley?"

"I do," Lieutenant Zabrinski said.

"If you should find him, or hear word of Adeline Hopkins, would you please contact me?"

"You have a card?" the lieutenant asked.

Ann nodded. She searched in her handbag for a business card and, once again, completed the ritual of crossing out Trevor Bowman's name before inserting her own. Yes, new business cards were an essential, she thought.

"Thank you," Lieutenant Zabrinski said as he accepted the business card.

"Thank *you*," Ann smiled.

"We're here to help," the lieutenant said. "After all, isn't that why we're in your country?"

"I appreciate your sacrifice," Ann said.

Lieutenant Zabrinski paused. He ran an eye over Ann, assessing her as a woman, as a person and, she wondered, as a detective? At the end of his deliberations he said, "I'm sure you do."

In silence, they walked through the sand dunes,

back to the army camp. With their feet resting on deeply engrained tracks, legacies of the heavy tanks, Lieutenant Zabrinski said, "Conversely, if you should encounter Sergeant Henley..."

"I'll get word to you."

Lieutenant Zabrinski smiled. He offered Ann a polite bow then said, "A pleasure to meet you, Mrs Morgan. I wish you good luck with your enquiry."

"A pleasure to meet you too, lieutenant. I wish you and your men good luck, when the time comes."

CHAPTER FIVE

Ann decided to widen her search, to the dance halls and stores of Bridgend. However, no one had seen or heard of Adeline Hopkins, or Sergeant Henley, for that matter. Perplexed, she returned to her allotment to release her frustration.

While tending the rhubarb, she spied a car, a bottle-green Austin 10. A smartly dressed man stepped out of the car – Charles Montagu.

In his early fifties, Montagu was tall and lean with a poker-straight back. He possessed intelligent brown eyes, a bulbous nose and a finely trimmed moustache. A pipe resided in his left-hand top pocket, a pipe he never seemed to smoke, while a pink carnation decorated his buttonhole. He paused to sniff the carnation. Then he smiled at Ann. Eager for news of Emrys, she placed her hoe in the ground and ran towards Montagu.

"Any word of Emrys?" she asked.

"No, I'm afraid not, old girl." Montagu placed his hands behind his back. He shook his head in weary fashion. "However, no need for additional worry; it's chaotic on the Continent, difficult for anyone to get word through. This is the decisive push. Once the Nazis start to retreat, the game will be up." He glanced over Ann's shoulder to the potatoes, carrots and rhubarb. "You are keeping busy, I see."

"With the allotment," Ann said.

"And with a little sleuthing, I hear."

"How do you know that?" Ann frowned.

Montagu tapped the side of his nose. He grinned. "It's my business to know these things, my dear." Displaying a dancer's grace, he turned to view the sand dunes, the army camp and the ships far out to sea. The ships were laden with essential supplies and, to watching eyes, they seemed to take forever to crawl to the shore.

"Are you thinking of making the detective agency your full time career?" Montagu asked, his gaze returning to Ann.

"I'm in two minds," she said truthfully. "Sometimes, the idea appeals to me; then, I struggle with doubts."

Montagu nodded. He said, "Maybe you should offer the detective agency some serious thought."

"Do you think I could do it?"

"You're a resourceful woman," Montagu said, "with an abundance of talent; I think you'd be up for the task. Besides," he smiled, "an occupation like that would occupy your mind. And, who knows, in the future, you could even assist me with covert enquires."

"Spy on people?" Ann frowned.

"Not spy, exactly," Montagu said. "But that's

for the future. What of the present?"

"I'm looking for a runaway, a farm worker, Adeline Hopkins."

Montagu puckered his lips. He shook his head. "Can't say I've heard of her."

"She might be with a GI, Sergeant Glenn Henley."

"Can't say I've heard of him either."

"If you were searching for them," Ann asked, "where would you look?"

Montagu paused. He leaned back on his heels. He wore black and white spats today and through his clothing and balletic movements, Ann sensed that he'd missed his calling – he really should have been a dancer.

"Do you think that Adeline and Sergeant Henley are together?" Montagu asked.

"It's a possibility," Ann said.

Montagu nodded. He removed his pipe from his top pocket and examined the stem. Maybe that's why he carried the pipe, Ann mused, as an aid to concentration. The spymaster scrutinized the stem as though studying a rare jewel. He offered a secret smile then said, "First, they would require shelter, a place with a roof over their heads. And they would require food. With his uniform and accent, Sergeant Henley would stick out like a sore thumb, so a public place would be out of the question. They would seek somewhere private, an isolated spot next to nature's pantry and fresh water."

"An abandoned building," Ann said.

"An old barn," Montagu suggested, "a deserted cottage, an old mill..."

"Next to running water."

Montagu nodded. He placed his pipe in his left-hand top pocket and tapped the bowl. "If I were you, old girl, I'd follow the river."

Ann smiled at the term 'old girl', a favourite of Charles Montagu's. However, she had yet to experience her twenty-seventh birthday. A melancholy thought washed over her – would she celebrate that day alone?

Nevertheless, she forced up a smile and said, "Thank you, Charles."

"Any time, old girl. And chin up; keep thinking of Emrys."

How could she forget him; how could she think of anything else? Yet she must, she told herself. She had a job to do. With or without melancholy thoughts, life would go on.

Ann walked with Charles Montagu, back to his Austin 10. At the car, they paused again, to look at the American soldiers.

"I wonder what they're thinking," Ann said.

"Shall I tell you what I was thinking," Montagu said, "the day I boarded my ship to face the Hun in the Great War?"

"What were you thinking?" Ann asked.

"I was thinking, I hope I lose my virginity before this ship goes down."

"And did you?" Ann smiled.

Montagu laughed. He climbed into his car and winked at Ann, "I've said too much. Yet, maybe, I haven't said enough. It's a story I'll save for another day."

CHAPTER SIX

Ann followed the River Kenfig, upstream, from the ruins of the medieval castle to the old mill at Llanmihangel. On the 20th August 1940 while aiming for industrial targets, the Luftwaffe dropped four bombs near the castle. All the bombs exploded leaving a crater a hundred yards long, ten yards wide and ten yards deep. That crater was still visible. The following day, the Luftwaffe bombed the RAF airfield at Stormy Down, then they left well alone. Although Ann was no military strategist, she often wondered about Hitler's tactics. Did he regard those attacks as failures? Did he become bored and seek to strike elsewhere? Did he lack the resources to sustain the attacks? Was he insane? Yes, he was definitely insane, and through his insanity, he would fall. Also, Ann noted, when the Luftwaffe attacked the local area it brought the people closer together; it strengthened their resolve, and that too would ensure Hitler's downfall.

Ann picked her way through the brambles, shrubs and trees, to Water Street. At Water Street, she examined an old barn, but saw no sign of life. She took a detour, towards an old cottage, but again the building was devoid of life.

Ann crossed the railway line and stared down at Llanmihangel Mill. The mill dated from 1186 when the monks at Margam used its power to grind their corn. Ann's father, a keen local historian, had told her a story about the mill. In 1358, Brother Meuric, a lay brother, was indicted for harbouring two men at the mill, John ap Griffith and Rees ap Griffith, brothers and felons. In his defence, Brother Meuric opted for trial at an ecclesiastical court, where he was acquitted.

After the Dissolution of the Monasteries in 1536, the mill fell into private hands. Over the centuries, it declined, grinding the last of its corn in 1926. Would Ann find Adeline Hopkins or Sergeant Glenn Henley at the mill? Outside the building, she discovered warm ashes from a camp fire. Therefore, she moved inside, to investigate.

Ann glanced around the dusty mill, at the fallen masonry and the old millstones. As she examined the curved, worn surface of a millstone, a woman entered the building, Adeline Hopkins. Ann recognized Adeline from brief meetings around town and the occasions she had called at her father's farm for honey and eggs.

"What are you doing here?" Adeline asked. She took a step back, towards the door, which hung at a drunken angle, on one hinge.

"I've been looking for you," Ann said. "Your mother is concerned about you."

"And my father?" Adeline frowned.

"You don't get on with him."

"You can say that again," she sighed.

Adeline flopped on to a large limestone block that, with the aid of a canvas sack, she had fashioned into a makeshift chair.

"Why don't you get on with him?"

"He's too strict," Adeline said. "I'm never good enough for him."

"But you do get on with your mother."

Adeline raised her left shoulder and offered a diffident shrug. With her right hand, she adjusted her crêpe dress, which contained a tear along the shoulder. While fingering the tear, she said, "My mother's all right. She's too soft; she'll do anything for a quiet life."

Ann nodded. She took a moment to study Adeline. The young woman possessed long auburn hair, blue eyes, a full figure and countless freckles, which dotted her arms and face. Since their previous meeting, she had put on a few extra pounds in weight, which suggested that the farm had increased its production to supplement the family's rations.

Adeline's crêpe dress was smart, Ann noted, a party outfit. Originally pale blue, she had dyed the dress a vivid shade of lavender to freshen up her wardrobe.

"Why did you run away?" Ann asked.

"I needed time to think."

"About your father?"

Adeline offered Ann a guarded sideways glance. Then she turned away. "And other things."

"How have you coped?"

"There's fresh water in the river," Adeline said, "and plenty of food in the woods."

"You've been scavenging?"

She nodded. "I've done that since childhood. If you know what you're looking for, you can survive."

Adeline paused to adjust the tear in her dress. As she fingered the tear, moisture brightened her eyes.

"What happened to your dress?" Ann asked.

"I caught it," Adeline said, "on a branch."

In need of fresh air, Adeline walked out of the mill. Ann followed her, to the riverbank.

While gazing at the clear water, Ann said, "You mentioned that you came here to think about other things, besides your father."

"My ex-boyfriend," Adeline said. She plucked a daisy from the grass and twirled the flower between her fingers.

"Richard Lyall?"

"Yes." Adeline turned abruptly to face Ann. She frowned, "Have you met him?"

"I have," Ann said.

"He's like my father," Adeline said, "too aggressive, too demanding." She sighed, a breath drawn up from the soles of her platform shoes. "I always seem to attract the aggressive types."

"And you are similar to your mother; you want a quiet life."

"Is that too much to ask," Adeline groaned, "even with a war on?"

"Are you still walking out with Richard?" Ann asked.

"No," Adeline said wiping the tears from her eyes, "I told you, he's my ex; it's over."

"What about Sergeant Glenn Henley?"

Adeline's eyes widened. She viewed Ann with deep suspicion. "What do you know about him?" she asked.

"I understand that you were walking out with Sergeant Henley, for a short time."

"I met him at a dance," Adeline said, her back turned towards Ann. "But nothing came of it. We didn't walk out together."

"Richard intervened?"

"Yes," she said in a small voice.

"Richard had words with Sergeant Henley?"

"Yes," she said.

"And a fight?"

"They threw punches at each other. They brawled. But even without that, Glenn wasn't for me. And I told him so."

"Glenn was too aggressive?"

Adeline turned to face Ann. She mumbled, "Like I said, I attract those types."

"Have you seen him lately?"

"Glenn?"

"Yes."

"No," Adeline said. She gazed at the daisy, which had wilted between her fingers. "Why do you ask?"

"He's gone missing."

Adeline dropped the daisy into the river where it floated above the sticklebacks and minnows. "I don't know anything about that," she said.

Ann followed Adeline back to the mill. With food from the forest and water from the stream, Adeline could survive. True, her creature comforts were limited. However, her surroundings compared favourably with the satanic landscapes of the bombed-out cities.

"What would you like to do?" Ann asked.

"Stay here," Adeline said, "and think."

"May I tell your mother that you're safe?"

Adeline paused. She straightened the pleats on her party dress. Despite the vivid lavender dye, the dress retained its pre-war look, a reminder of more innocent days.

"Okay," Adeline said, "but don't tell my

mother, or my father, where I am."

Ann nodded. She took a step away from the mill then said, "I'll call again soon, if that's all right with you. Is there anything you want?"

"Nothing," Adeline said. "All I want is some peace and quiet, and some time alone."

CHAPTER SEVEN

The following morning, Ann woke up to the sound of birds chirping outside her bedroom window and the warmth of sunlight as it kissed her feather pillow. Automatically, she rolled over to face Emrys but, of course, he wasn't there.

Ann stretched. Then she jumped out of bed and wandered over to the window. Through the window, she noticed a commotion on the sand dunes with a line of people, including police officers, walking to the coast.

After a brief detour to the bathroom to wash her face, and to her wardrobe to select her clothes, she ran across the sand dunes to investigate.

On the sand dunes, Ann made her way to the coast where she found Detective Inspector Max Deveraux and Lieutenant Mike Zabrinski. She waited while the two men talked in earnest fashion. Eventually, she captured Deveraux's attention and the weary detective limped towards her.

"What happened?" Ann asked.

"We found a GI, washed up on the shore."

"Sergeant Glenn Henley?"

Deveraux offered Ann a suspicious stare. He rolled his trilby between his fingers and said, "You are well informed."

"Is he dead?" Ann asked.

"Yes," Deveraux said.

"How did he die?"

"Sergeant Henley has bruises all over his body and a number of broken bones. At a guess, he fell on to the rocks and was swept out to sea."

Ann glanced up to the rocky escarpment. The cliffs were not particularly tall at this point along the coast; however, they were high enough to demand caution.

"And now the tide has washed him back in," Ann said.

She stepped aside as two police officers carried the soldier's body, on a stretcher, towards the army camp. Grey blankets covered the body, offering a degree of decorum.

"Did he fall," Ann asked, "or was he pushed?"

"That's to be determined," Deveraux said.

Deveraux and Lieutenant Zabrinski conferred once more, out of Ann's earshot. Then the detective inspector talked with two men, a detective sergeant and a police driver. At the close of their conversation, Deveraux asked Ann, "What do you know about Sergeant Henley?"

"Nothing," Ann said. "I saw the commotion from my bedroom window and ran out to investigate."

"That instinct comes naturally to you," Deveraux said his fingers brushing an imaginary speck from his trilby.

Ann frowned. She thought about his comment then said, "I guess it does."

Ann followed Deveraux along the beach. From the damp sand, they studied the cliff face and the jagged rocks, the granite-hard boulders that had claimed Glenn Henley's life. Uniformed policemen milled around, searching for evidence, looking for clues, while local men and women gathered on the cliff top and the beach; drawn like moths to the flame, they were captivated by the scene.

Amongst the locals, Ann spied a number of soldiers from the 28th Infantry Division. She wondered what they made of the tragedy. Her mind went back a month to June when three American soldiers had drowned while swimming in Kenfig Pool. Had Sergeant Glenn Henley succumbed to a similar accident?

With his gaze on the seaweed-strewn rocks, Deveraux asked, "Did you find Adeline Hopkins?"

Ann paused. She swept her honey-blonde hair from her eyes. Although it was a bright, sunny day, the sea breeze was fresh. Then she looked Deveraux in the eye and decided to lie. The lie disturbed her. However, she had promised Adeline that, for the time being, she would not reveal her whereabouts. "I'm still looking," Ann said.

Deveraux nodded accepting her word. He said,

"I understand that Adeline walked out with Henley, the victim."

"It was only a dalliance," Ann said; "they didn't walk out together."

Deveraux narrowed his tired brown eyes. He squinted at Ann with some suspicion. "How do you know that?" he asked.

"Just local gossip," Ann said with the colour rising on her cheeks. "Through listening to people in the shops, at the dance halls," she added hastily.

Deveraux stared at Ann. He arched a suspicious eyebrow. With restless fingers, he twirled his trilby, spun the hat around in his large hands.

"When you catch up with Adeline," he said, "I'd like a word with her."

"Of course," Ann said. "When I catch up with Adeline, I'll inform you."

Deveraux nodded. He took a step away from Ann. Then he turned and said, "Oh, I nearly forgot; you owe me a favour."

Ann frowned. Her duplicity had left her feeling confused. "I'm sorry?" she said.

"Over the incident on the sand dunes; the rogue gunner. I thought that maybe you could join me in a picnic."

"I'd like that," Ann said. She smiled, a gesture blessed with warmth and affection.

Deveraux placed his trilby on his head. He gave the hat a contented tap. "Be seeing you," he said.

As Detective Inspector Deveraux walked away, to rejoin his colleagues, Lieutenant Mike Zabrinski strolled towards Ann.

"A terrible business," he said, concern clouding his clean-cut, handsome features. "What should I tell his parents?"

"An accident?" Ann suggested. "Suicide?"

"Not the type," Lieutenant Zabrinski said shaking his head.

"Maybe he argued with someone at the camp and they pushed him on to the rocks?"

Zabrinski ran his fingers through his short dark hair. He looked out to sea, his expression grim. "That's possible, I suppose. The men are all hyped-up, ready to move out. Tensions and emotions are running high."

"But," Ann said, "you suspect another motive."

Zabrinski nodded. "If one of my men did this, word would get around. We're a tight-knit group, and I haven't heard anything, yet."

"Therefore," Ann surmised, "you suspect a local."

The lieutenant offered Ann a wide smile, as bright and white as a toothpaste advertisement. He said, "You catch on fast, ma'am." With his expression serious he added, "I believe Glenn had an argument with a trainee gunner, Richard Lyall?"

"Do you think Lyall killed him?"

"I understand they traded punches. If I were in Detective Inspector Deveraux's shoes, I reckon I'd want a word with Richard Lyall. What do you reckon, ma'am?"

Ann turned and stared inland towards Stormy Down. "Lieutenant Zabrinski," she said, "I reckon you're right."

CHAPTER EIGHT

From the beach at Kenfig, Ann drove to Stormy Down in search of Richard Lyall. She had to wait half an hour while he completed his training. Then she caught up with him in the dining hall. Largely alone, he sat in the centre of the wooden hall, at a trestle table, drinking a cup of tea, scoffing a meal of spam and powdered eggs.

"Sorry I can't offer you anything," Richard Lyall said with a grin, "service personnel and families only."

"That's okay," Ann said, although in truth she found the bland spam and powdered eggs enticing, a reminder that she had skipped breakfast and lunch. "Do you mind if I sit down?" she asked.

"Be my guest," Lyall said, waving his fork towards a straight-backed wooden chair.

Ann sat on the chair, opposite Lyall. She straightened the pleats on her skirt then asked, "A successful practice mission?"

"The guns worked like a dream," Lyall said while shovelling forkfuls of food.

Ann offered a thin smile. She stared at Lyall then asked, "Do you dream of killing people?"

Lyall sat back. Instinctively, his fingers tightened around his fork. Meanwhile, he chewed on his spam and powdered eggs. He swallowed the food, washed it down with a sip of tea, then said, "I think about it. But I don't dream about it, or have nightmares for that matter. We're at war; it's my job."

"And after the war," Ann asked, "will you continue to fly?"

"I love being up there, free in the fresh air. Yeah, if possible, I'll continue to fly."

"And what about Adeline?" Ann asked. "Do you picture her in your future?"

Lyall placed his fork on his plate. He stared at Ann through dark, brooding eyes. "She ditched me," he said. "It's over."

"But you still have feelings for her."

Lyall reached for a side plate. On the plate, he found a thick slice of brown bread. He folded the bread over and proceeded to mop a sliver of grease from his dinner plate. He chewed on the bread. Then, with a shrug, he said, "I guess I do; I guess she meant something to me."

"You argued with Sergeant Glenn Henley," Ann said.

"I admitted that," Lyall scowled; "I told you."

"Sergeant Henley is dead."

"I know," Lyall said; "it's the talk of the camp."

"You punched him," Ann said.

"I told you that too."

"Did you murder him?"

Lyall reached for his mug of muddy-brown tea. He stared into its tepid depths, searched for the tealeaves within the unsweetened liquid. "For what reason?" he asked.

"Your feelings for Adeline."

With some force, he slammed his mug on to the trestle table. The table shook while the lukewarm tea stained its surface. "Do you think I'm some sort of nutter," he asked, "someone who enjoys violence?"

Ann glanced at a knot of airmen who had gathered beside the canteen door. She offered them an apologetic smile. Then she said to Lyall, "I don't think you're a nutter, but I do think violence comes easy to you."

"Okay," he sighed, sitting back, staring at a rivulet of tea as it snaked its way over the scarred wooden surface, as it followed the grooves in the trestle table, "so I have an aggressive streak, but I didn't kill the Yank soldier."

"Who did?" Ann asked.

"I don't know," Lyall said. "But I'm telling you straight, it wasn't me."

Ann shuffled in her seat. She moved her legs, to avoid the dripping tea. Meanwhile, Lyall had regained his composure, so she asked, "How did Sergeant Henley end up in the sea?"

"I guess he slipped and fell off the cliff."

"When drunk?"

Lyall shrugged. "Yeah, that's a possibility."

"Was Sergeant Henley drunk when you punched him?"

Lyall laughed. "Yeah, he'd swigged one or two too many. From what the lads said, he was always drunk, always swigging one or two too many."

"And the alcohol made him aggressive?"

"It made him aggressive and randy. Although," Lyall laughed again, "from what I've seen, it doesn't take much to make these Yanks randy."

Ann stood. She smiled at Richard Lyall. "Thank you," she said. "And I hope you fulfil your dream, after the war."

Lyall stood. He walked with Ann, into the compound. There, he said, "No hard feelings about the stray bullets."

"No hard feelings," Ann said, her words sincere, crystalline in their truth. With her mind on Sergeant Glenn Henley and a solution to his murder she added, "No hard feelings at all."

CHAPTER NINE

From the airfield at Stormy Down, Ann returned to Llanmihangel Mill and Adeline Hopkins. En route, she gazed at the local villages and recalled the night in May 1941 when an enemy bomb had destroyed the porch of St Theodore's church. Seven months earlier, a bomb had landed in a farmer's field, but failed to explode.

Ann also gazed west to the devastated town of Swansea. In February 1941, during a three-night blitz, the Luftwaffe had destroyed the town and docks, and claimed far too many lives. Over those three nights, the destruction of water mains made the fire-fighters' task virtually impossible. Indeed, many miles of hose stretched from the North and South Docks in a desperate attempt to maintain a supply of water. During sunny, tranquil days, such horrors seemed a world away; yet the scars remained, and would never fade.

At Llanmihangel Mill, Ann found Adeline sitting beside the river. While kneeling on the grass, she asked, "How are you?"

Adeline picked at her torn dress. She shrugged. "I'm okay."

"I've been talking with Richard Lyall."

"How is he?" Adeline asked, her tone flat, her gaze distant.

"He's fine," Ann said. She paused and watched as insects hovered over the river, their gossamer wings glinting in the sunlight. The image invoked memories of childhood, of jam jars crammed with tadpoles, of running carefree amongst the sand dunes, of chasing butterflies, in vain. With a sigh, Ann's thoughts returned to Adeline. While gazing at the young woman, she asked, "Do you have any regrets over parting with Richard?"

"A few pangs," she conceded, "occasionally; but he wasn't for me."

Ann sat on the grass, beside Adeline. Meanwhile, the river trickled by. As the water flowed over sand and stone, it created a natural melody, harmonious and soothing. In that moment, Ann understood why Adeline had sought the riverside as a sanctuary, in her quest to ease her troubled mind.

To the sound of a cow, mooing in the distance, Ann asked, "When was the last time you saw Sergeant Henley?"

"A few nights ago," Adeline mumbled, "I think."

"Just before you took refuge at the mill?"

"Around that time, yes."

"You saw him at a dance?"

"Yes."

"Was he drunk at the dance?"

Adeline turned and stared at Ann, her eyes wide, troubled with suspicion. She said in a quiet voice, "He'd been drinking heavily, yes."

"The cliffs can be dangerous when you're drunk."

"They can be," Adeline agreed.

"Men can be dangerous when they're drunk."

Adeline stood up. She walked away from Ann. Over her shoulder, she called out, "I don't know what you mean."

"Sometimes," Ann said, "they won't take no for an answer."

Adeline ran, into the mill. Ann scurried after her.

Ann found Adeline in the mill, sobbing her heart out. "I don't know what you're saying," Adeline said between sniffles.

"I think you do," Ann said.

Ann walked over to Adeline and placed a hand on her shoulder, her fingers covering the tear in the troubled woman's dress.

"I'm not here to punish you," Ann said; "I'm here to help."

"No one can help me," Adeline said in a small voice.

Ann took hold of Adeline's hand. She guided her to the large limestone block, the makeshift chair covered with a canvas sack, and there they sat together.

As Adeline's sobs subsided, Ann asked, "What happened at the cliff top?"

"Sergeant Henley came on to me," Adeline said. "You're right, he wouldn't take no for an answer. After the dance, he gave me loads of presents...cigarettes, spam, chocolate, stockings, chewing gum. He'd come prepared. He'd loaded his pockets, as though he intended to buy me. I said, thanks, but no thanks. He said, he'd be leaving soon; he'd be joining the troops in France. He asked if I'd do him a favour. He said it was my patriotic duty."

"He kissed you," Ann said.

"And the rest," Adeline cried. "He ripped my clothes; he pawed me like an animal."

"He tore your dress."

"Yes," Adeline said.

"So you pushed him away."

"And he slipped," Adeline sobbed, "on the damp grass."

"He fell," Ann said, "over the cliff."

"Yes," Adeline nodded. "He fell into the sea. I thought the waves would sweep him away."

"The ebb tide washed him out," Ann said, "but the flow tide returned his body to the shore."

Adeline looked up, her blue eyes bright, her freckled face streaked with tears. "I didn't murder him," she said. "I mean, I didn't mean to do it. I just pushed him away." She buried her face in her hands and sobbed, her shoulders shaking uncontrollably.

When Adeline had used up all her tears, she turned to Ann and asked, "What happens now?"

"I'm not sure," Ann said. She stood and took hold of Adeline's hand. "But you can't stay here. I think you should come with me."

Chapter Ten

Ann escorted Adeline to Homestead cottage. There, she offered the young woman a meal cultivated from her allotment – a dish of potatoes and a vegetable pie, washed down with a cup of tea. After four days of eating leaves and berries, Adeline was grateful for the meal and, despite her perilous position, she cleared her plate.

While Adeline distracted her mind with copies of *Vogue* and *Picture Post*, Ann walked to the army camp in search of Lieutenant Mike Zabrinski. She found him amongst a hive of activity. Indeed, the soldiers were on the verge of leaving. However, despite his busy schedule, Lieutenant Zabrinski agreed to accompany Ann to Homestead cottage.

Adeline looked up as Ann and Zabrinski entered. She placed the magazines on a coffee table, her face a mask of concern.

"This is Lieutenant Zabrinski," Ann said. Noting Adeline's distress, she kept her tone as light as possible, underpinned with a smile of reassurance; "he's a liaison officer. Please tell him what you told me."

Adeline stood. She backed away, into a corner. "But..." she stumbled, "he'll go to the police."

"I'm asking you to trust me," Ann said, "and Lieutenant Zabrinski. In truth, you have no alternative because, sooner or later, the police will find their way to your door."

Adeline sighed. Her gaze wandered from Ann to Lieutenant Zabrinski. Acknowledging her predicament, she sat and said, "Okay, if you insist."

Through a veil of tears, Adeline recalled the cliff top incident. At the close of her story, Ann offered her a handkerchief, to dry her eyes. She waited until Adeline had regained some of her composure. Then she accompanied Lieutenant Zabrinski into the front garden.

In the garden, while standing amongst the roses, Ann said, "If we inform the police, it would be embarrassing for your unit, and devastating for Adeline; there would be a trial and she might face the hangman."

Zabrinski caressed his square jaw. He grimaced. "We're taking her at her word?"

"Do you doubt her?" Ann asked.

He glanced through the living room window into the shadows. Adeline sat in those shadows, a melancholy figure, her features gaunt, her mind in turmoil.

"I don't doubt her," Lieutenant Zabrinski said. "I believe she's telling the truth."

Ann nodded. She said, "You strike me as a man of honour, Lieutenant Zabrinski; as a man of honour, do you believe that Adeline should face the hangman?"

Grim-faced, he shook his head and said, "I do not, ma'am."

Ann walked with Lieutenant Zabrinski, along her garden path, to her front gate. From the gate, she stared into the army camp. Vehicles were rolling out – tanks, jeeps and DUKWs. Soldiers were marching, thousands of men in regular columns, to join the invasion. Soon, they would board ships and land in France. After nearly five years of fighting, the crucial moment had arrived, the decisive battle of the war. Ann's temporary neighbours, good-natured men, cheerful in the face of adversity, would depart these shores. Ann's heart went with them, along with her hopes.

With a sigh, she turned to Lieutenant Zabrinski and said, "I understand that many soldiers have stood in Sergeant Henley's shoes, and many local women have been placed in Adeline's position."

Lieutenant Zabrinski watched as the soldiers filed past, aware that within the hour he would join them. "My men are on their way to France, to engage with the enemy. Many will not return; do you blame them?"

"I do not condemn their passion," Ann said, "but even in times of war we must still hold on to a sense of decency and reason."

Once again, the handsome soldier caressed his

square jaw. He turned to Ann and asked, "So, ma'am, what's the solution?"

"We could inform the police," Ann said. "They would arrest Adeline and that would lead to a trial. At a guess, an all male jury would side with Sergeant Henley and Adeline would face the hangman. Meanwhile, you would have to write to Sergeant Henley's parents to explain how their son met his tragic end. In this case, maybe justice would be served if Adeline reflected on the tragedy and learned from the bitter experience, and if you informed Sergeant Henley's parents that their son died in a dreadful accident while serving his country."

"We lie to protect the guilty," Zabrinski said.

"No," Ann said. "We bend the truth to protect two people who, at heart, are innocents."

Zabrinski nodded. He offered Ann a thoughtful look. "A scandal would not honour the division or endear our men to the locals."

Ann concurred. She said, "You leave these shores with our good wishes, and our high hopes. You leave behind fond memories; why tarnish any of that?"

Lieutenant Zabrinski stood to attention, his mind made up. "I will contact Detective Inspector Deveraux and inform him accordingly. My investigations suggest that Sergeant Henley met with a tragic accident."

Ann smiled at Lieutenant Mike Zabrinski. With hope in her voice she said, "Come back to us, safe and sound."

In turn, the lieutenant offered Ann a broad grin and a sharp salute. "Ma'am," he said, "I intend to."

CHAPTER ELEVEN

Ann drove Adeline home to Marshfield Farm. There, her mother embraced her while her father looked on, his features stern, his expression grim. Adeline had escaped the hangman. However, she would have to endure her father's wrath, and live with the consequences of her actions. Her path would not be a smooth one. Indeed, Ann foresaw a road strewn with stones. Nevertheless, if Adeline could endure the present and overcome future obstacles, she would emerge as a stronger, better person.

With that thought in mind, Ann returned to Homestead cottage where she found Detective Inspector Max Deveraux waiting on her doorstep.

"I've talked with Lieutenant Zabrinski," Deveraux said, his tone curt, businesslike.

"About Sergeant Henley?"

"Yes. It seems the Americans are happy to regard Sergeant Henley's death as an accident."

"Well," Ann shrugged, "I suppose that's a solution, of sorts."

Deveraux removed his trilby. He spun the hat around on his fingers in agitated fashion. He glared at Ann. "What information did you pass on to Lieutenant Zabrinski?"

"Information?" Ann asked with an innocent smile.

"Don't lie to me, Ann." The use of her first name caught Ann by surprise, and she sucked in a deep breath. With the devil in his eyes, Deveraux said, "I know you well enough by now; I know when you're lying, and when you're telling the truth."

Two spots of red flared on Ann's cheeks. She sensed the tension in the air, akin to an impending storm. With anger in her voice, she said, "You'd swear that we were walking out together."

"Maybe we should," Deveraux suggested.

"No," Ann said, turning away. "I love my husband."

Deveraux nodded. He sighed. Then he spoke with contrition in his voice. "Please forgive me if I've talked out of turn, but I thought we had an understanding."

"We do," Ann said.

"I thought we were friends."

"We are."

"Then how about sharing the truth?" Deveraux frowned. "What happened to Henley?"

Ann glanced over her shoulder to the army camp. A group of soldiers remained. However, the camp was largely deserted.

"The Americans are happy to close the case,"

Ann said. "They're on their way to France. Maybe we should respect their wishes and let bygones be bygones."

"I see," Deveraux said with a scowl.

"I hope you do."

"You won't tell me."

Ann sighed. She said, "My words would only inflame open wounds."

Deveraux placed his trilby on his head. He offered the hat a firm tap, adjusted the brim, then walked away from Ann. "Maybe we should take a rain check on the picnic."

"I understand," Ann said.

Deveraux climbed into his car, a black Wolseley. With his eyes on the road, he said, "I'll see you around."

Ann watched Max Deveraux depart with a heavy heart. She felt upset because she had deceived him over Adeline, and distressed because he was angry with her. Later, she endured a restless night with little sleep.

CHAPTER TWELVE

The sound of an engine woke Ann. At first, she thought the noise emanated from an aeroplane. Then she realised that it originated from a car. She stretched, reached for her dressing gown and wandered over to the bedroom window.

Peering through the window, Ann recognized Charles Montagu's bottle-green Austin 10. Dragging her fingers through her hair, she ran downstairs to open the front door. There, looking as fresh as a daisy and as dapper as ever, she found Charles Montagu on her doorstep.

"Good morning," Montagu said. He stooped to retrieve a milk bottle.

"Emrys," Ann said; whenever she saw Charles, her thoughts went to Emrys.

"May I step inside?" Montagu asked.

"But of course," Ann said.

Montagu handed Ann the milk bottle and she placed it in the kitchen. Then he followed her into the living room. There, he offered her a folded sheet of paper. Ann unfurled the paper. She stared at five lines, at five rows of ciphers and symbols.

"We received this message," Montagu said, "in the early hours of the morning."

"It doesn't make any sense," Ann frowned.

Montagu chuckled. "It won't, old girl, at least to

you. It's coded. But it's signed with Emrys' codename. At this stage, we don't know where he is; as I told you earlier, it's chaotic over there; but he's alive, and now we know that for certain."

"Alive," Ann said, moistening her lips, savouring the word. "Emrys is alive."

"And further good news," Montagu said. He paused to sniff his carnation, which adorned his buttonhole. "Keep this under your hat, my dear, this is top, top secret, but according to reports, someone tried to assassinate Hitler."

"Did they get him?" Ann gasped.

"We don't know about that. But the cracks are widening. The war will soon be over."

"And Emrys will be home," Ann said.

Montagu nodded. "Once the Americans land in Normandy, they'll clear a path through France and Emrys will find a way back to you." The spymaster placed his hands behind his back. He raised himself up, on to his toes, and glanced towards the kitchen. "Maybe you should check your tea caddy and polish your kettle," he suggested. "When Emrys returns, I'm sure he'll be desperate for a brew."

With Ann in a daze, Charles Montagu returned to his Austin 10. He pressed the car horn, enticed a squeak, then drove away.

Emrys was alive, Ann told herself. She repeated the phrase, over and over again. Emrys was alive.

She ran into the kitchen and filled the kettle. She would make a brew. And the tea would taste like champagne.

Web Links

For details about Hannah Howe and her books, please visit https://hannah-howe.com

To listen to audio book samples from Hannah's books please visit https://hananh-howe.com/audiobooks

Praise for Hannah Howe

"Hannah Howe is a very talented writer."

"I cannot recommend this author strongly enough."

"A gem of a read."

"Sam is an endearing character. Her assessments of some of the people she encounters will make you laugh at her wicked mind. At other times, you'll cry at the pain she's suffered."

"Sam is the kind of non-assuming heroine that I couldn't help but love."

"Sam's Song was a wonderful find and a thoroughly engaging read. The first book in the Sam Smith mystery series, this book starts off as a winner!"

"Sam is an interesting and very believable character."

"Gripping and believable at the same time, very well written."

"Hannah Howe is a fabulous writer."

"Sam is a great heroine who challenges stereotypes."

"I can't wait to read the next in the series!"

"The Big Chill is light reading, but packs powerful messages."

"This series just gets better and better."

"What makes this book stand well above the rest of detective thrillers is the attention to the little details that makes everything so real."

"Sam is a rounded and very real character."

"Howe is an author to watch, able to change the tone from light hearted to more thoughtful, making this an easy and yet very rewarding read. Cracking!"

"Fabulous book by a fabulous author – I highly recommended this series!"

"Howe writes her characters with depth and makes them very engaging."

"In Dr Alan Storey, the author has created a strong male character that is willing to take a step back and support Sam in her career decisions because that's what she needs to grow stronger. I definitely recommend this series."

"I loved Hannah Howe's writing style — poignant one moment, terrifying the next, funny the next moment. I would be on the edge of my seat praying Sam wouldn't get hurt, and then she'd say a one-liner or think something funny, and I'd chuckle and catch my breath. Love it!"

"Sam's Song is no lightweight suspense book. Howe deals with drugs, spousal abuse, child abuse, and more. While the topics she writes about are heavy, Howe does a fantastic job of giving the reader the brutal truth while showing us there is still good in life and hope for better days to come."

"What's special about Sam's Song? It's well written: accomplished, witty, at times ironical, and economical. A lot of the impact comes from Hannah Howe's ability to achieve effects in a paragraph that many writers spend a page over."

"I loved the easy conversational style the author used throughout. Some of the colourful ways that the main character expressed herself actually made me laugh!"

"Sam's Song is more than a standard private detective novel. It has real characters, not stereotypes and it treats those characters with compassion and wit."

"If you love empowered women sleuths, you must read the Sam Smith Mystery Series now."

About the Author

Hannah Howe is the author of the Sam Smith Mystery Series, a series that has reached #1 on the Amazon private investigator's chart on five separate occasions. Hannah also writes the Ann's War Mystery Series and stand-alone novels.

Hannah's books are available in print, as eBooks and audio books from all major outlets, including iBooks, Barnes and Noble, Smashwords, Amazon, Kobo and Audible.

Hannah lives in Glamorgan, Wales with her family. Her interests include reading, music, genealogy, chess and classic black and white movies.